A Kingfisher Read-Alone

ZOOM
ON A BROOM!
Six fun-filled stories

Judy Hindley

ILLUSTRATED BY
TONI GOFFE

Kingfisher Books
NEW YORK

KINGFISHER BOOKS
Grisewood & Dempsey Inc.
95 Madison Avenue
New York, New York 10016

First American Edition 1992

2 4 6 8 10 9 7 5 3 1

Text copyright © Judith Hindley 1991
Illustrations copyright © Toni Goffe 1991

A *Kingfisher Read-Alone* is a trademark of
Kingfisher Books, Grisewood & Dempsey Inc.

Library of Congress Catalog Card Number: 92–053100
CIP Data applied for

ISBN 1–85697–826–5

Printed in Spain

CONTENTS

The Magical Apple Tree

Rosy lived
with a mean old wicked witch.
The witch did nothing at all
but count her money.

Rosy did all the work.

She fed the hens
that laid eggs
for the witch.

She fed the cow
that gave milk
to the witch.

She fed the horse
that pulled the cart
that carried the wood
for the witch's fire.

All summer
she grew wheat and hay and oats
to fill the barns
for the animals' winter food.

But the witch
sold the wheat and hay and oats
and kept the money.

When winter came,
there was no food
in the barns.

The hens were so hungry
they laid no more eggs.

The cow was so hungry
it gave no more milk.

And the poor old horse
was too weak
to pull the cart.

The witch said,
"YOU'RE NO USE,
NOW."

"Tomorrow morning
the hens will go
in the cooking pot,
and the cow will go
to the butcher.
That old horse can go
wherever it likes –
and so can you!"

She kicked Rosy out
into the snow
and slammed the door.
Then she laughed
her wicked laugh,
"Caw, caw, caw!"
just like a mean old crow.

Rosy cried,
but the hungry animals
gathered around her.

So she said,
"I must go on.
After all, crying won't help,
and trying *might* help."
She picked up her empty basket
and went away
into the cold, bare woods.

Rosy walked and walked
till she came to
an apple tree.
It called to her.
In a sad, little voice
it cried,
"Please, dear Rosy,
shake me, shake me,
or this heavy fruit
will break me!"

Rosy looked up.
All she saw
was one dead leaf.
But the tree cried,
"Shake me, shake me!"
So she did.

10

Suddenly,
it was full of
yellow apples!
Rosy filled
her basket
and hurried home.

As she went,
the basket got
heavier and heavier.

But she didn't stop
for a minute
till she got home.

She poured out the fruit,
and the animals crowded around.

None of them saw
that the last five apples
had turned to gold.

But
the witch did.
"AHA!"
she cried.
"WHO
DID
YOU
ROB?"

"No one," said Rosy.
"I found these apples
in the woods.
There were lots and lots."

"LOTS?"
cried the witch.
And she rushed
into the woods.

Through the bare trees, the magical apple tree glimmered with fruit.

But the witch pushed past.

"Please," cried the apple tree, "shake me, shake me, or this heavy fruit will break me!"

But the witch said, "Pooh! I'm looking for *golden* apples. Shake yourself!"

So it did.
But this time,
the apples
turned into stones.

"Ow, ow, ow!"
cried the witch,
just like
a mean
old crow.
She hopped
and flapped
just like
a mean
old crow.

And suddenly
the wind
picked her up
and whirled her away.

And she never came back.

But Rosy sold the golden apples
and was rich!
And she and the animals
never went hungry again.

What do Witches Like?

What do witches
like to wear?
Big, black boots,

big, black capes,

big, black hats on their straggly hair!

What do witches like
to eat?

Fat rats,
boiled bats,

beetles, bugs, and spider stew –
what a treat!

What do witches
like to do?

Read a
magic
spell
book,

yell a
wicked yell,

brew a
magic
potion,

18

cast a
wicked
spell,

dance a wicked witch dance
in a magic ring,

ZOOM
on a broom, and

scare you!

BOO!

The Wonderful Turnip

Adam was a farmer.
He worked hard,
but for a long time,
nothing went right for him.

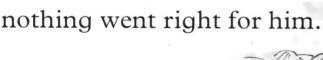

Hal, his brother,
was a soldier.
He had a fine, gray horse,
and a long, bright sword,
and lots of shiny buttons
on his uniform.
He was proud.

As time went by,
Adam got shabbier
and shabbier.

Hal did well.
Soon,
he had lots of medal
on his uniform.
When he saw Adam
he turned up his nos
and wouldn't
speak to him.

When Adam got married,
Hal rode by the church,
and didn't stop.
"Never mind,"
said Annie,
Adam's bride.
She said,
"Your luck
will change."
And it did.

22

That spring, Annie planted
a vegetable garden.
There were carrots and beans,
turnips and potatoes.
Everything grew well.
But the biggest plant of all
was a turnip.

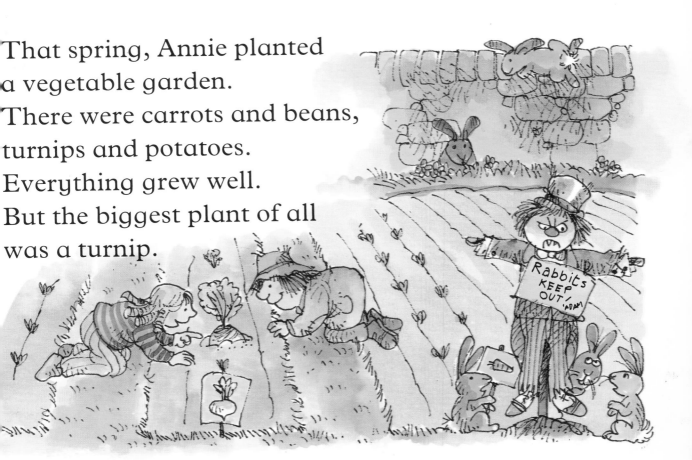

Adam said,
"Let's pull it up now,
and eat it!"
Only the little ones
are really tasty."
But Annie said,
"Let's wait.
It may be a special turnip."
So they waited.
And all summer long,
the turnip kept on growing.

It grew as high
as their middles,
and
it
kept
on
growing.

It grew as high
as their hats,
and
it
kept
on
growing.

It grew as high
as their apple tree,
and
it
still
kept
growing!

Every day,
more and more people came
to see the wonderful turnip.
Everybody came –
except for Hal.

Sometimes, Hal rode by
on his fine, gray horse,
but he turned up his nose
and never saw it.

25

Finally, Adam said,
"It's nearly winter.
We must pull up the turnip."
Everybody helped.
First, they dug and dug
to loosen the earth
around the turnip.
Then, they pulled,
and they pulled,
and they pulled,
and finally –

26

THUNK!

Out popped the turnip.
Adam said,
"We must take this turnip
to the king.
This is a king-sized turnip!"
So they did.

The king said,
"That's the biggest turnip
in the world!
I'll be famous!"
He was so happy,
he gave all his treasure
to Adam and Annie.

Adam and Annie
gave a wonderful party.
And the next time Hal rode by,
he stopped.

He said, "What happened?"
Did you find a treasure
in your turnip field?"

"Oh, no," said Adam.
"It came from the King.
We gave him our best turnip."
"Hmm," thought Hal.
"I can give him something bette
than a turnip!"
He sold his horse and sword
and medals and buttons,
and bought a wonderful jewel
for the king.

"What's this?" said the king.
"Another present!
What can I give to *you*?"
"Whatever you please,
Your Majesty," said Hal.
He thought,
"This silly king
will make me rich!"
"Wait here,"
said the king.
"I will bring you
the most special thing
I own.
It's only fair."

So Hal waited,
and he waited,
and he waited.
And at last,
here came
the king,
with . . .

THE TURNIP!

And what a rotten
old smelly turnip
it was!

Tricky Tom

Tom was clever.
He could tumble
and juggle
and do
magic tricks.
And he told
wonderful
fairy tales.

The princess
loved him.
She said,
"Ask my father
if you can
marry me."

So he did.

"Nonsense!"
said the king.
"Stick to your tricks,
Tom!"

But the next day
a giant
came to town
He stole things.
Everyone ran
from the giant.
No one
was brave enough
to face him.

Then the king
said to Tom,
"Here's your chance.
Get rid of
this giant,
and you can marry
the princess."

The princess
was terrified.
She cried
until
her handkerchief
was wet.
But Tom said,
"Don't cry –
I'll do it!"

So she gave him
her favorite bird
for luck,
and she gave him
her handkerchief,
though it was wet
with tears.

35

Tom went straight up
to the giant.
He said, "I've come
to tell you
to go away!"
Now really,
this giant
was a coward.
Tom startled him.
"Who are YOU?"
asked the giant,
trying to sound fierce.
"Do you know
what I could do to you?"
"Anything you can do,
I can do, too," said Tom.

"Huh!" said the giant.
"Watch this!
I can squeeze a stone
until it drips.
Just think
how I could squeeze
a silly boy!"
The giant
squeezed a stone
until it dripped.

"Pooh! said Tom.
"That's nothing!"
He pretended
to pick up a stone.
But really, he took out
the little wet handkerchief.
He squeezed, and squeezed,
and squeezed,
and of course –

37

it dripped.

"Huh!" said the giant.
"Well, watch this!
I can throw a stone
beyond that hill.
Just think
how I could throw
a silly boy!"

The giant
picked up a stone
and threw it
over the hill.

"Pooh!" said Tom.
"That's nothing!"
He pretended to pick up
another stone.
But really, he took out
the little bird.

He threw the bird
and it went right over the hill
and kept on going!

Then the giant said,
"Just you wait.
I'm going to pull up
this tree
and beat you with it!"

But once again,
Tom tricked him.

"Quick!"
cried Tom.
"Here comes a dragon!"

"Where!"
cried the cowardly giant.

"Follow me!"
Tom shouted.

They ran and ran and ran.

At last, Tom saw a barn
with a very big front door
and a small back window.

"Quick!" cried Tom.
"In here!"
He ran through
the big front door . . .

and jumped out
the small back window.

"Coming! Coming!"
cried the giant.

He ran
through
the big
front door,
and . . .

42

SMACK!

he ran
straight into
the wall.

43

Tom skipped around
and locked the front door
and trapped him.

The giant was beaten.
Tom took his boots
and all
his stolen loot,
and sent him away,
limping over the hills.

Then Tom went back
to the castle
and married the princess.
Everyone was glad.

Sometimes,
people asked him,
"How did you do it?"
Tom said,
"Let's go find another giant.
Then I'll show you!"

But they never did –
so nobody knows
but us.

The Fairy Harp

Some robbers
had a bad day.

One stole
a shiny
chain,

but
a dog
came with it.

One stole
a money box,

but
there was
nothing
in it.

One stole
a kettle,

but
it had
a hole.

Their fire went out.
"Oh, woe!"
cried
the robbers.

48

Everywhere they went,
something
stopped
them –
like a wall,
or a fence,
or a hedge.

That night,
as they rested,
they heard music.

Fairies were singing
to a harp.
They sang,
"Magic harp,
play us away –
over walls,
under fences,
down the streams,
through the hedges."

And it did.

WHOOSH!

51

"Hurray!" cried the robbers.
"Just what we need!"
They grabbed the harp
and sang,
"Magic harp,
play us away –
over walls,
under fences,
down the streams,
through the hedges."

And it did.

WHOOSH!
WHOMP!
CRASH!

After that,
one became
a butcher,

one became
a pie-man,

and one learned
to do repairs
on pots and kettles.

It suited them
much,
MUCH
better.

54

The Enchanted Princess

A beautiful princess named Gloriana
was riding in the mountains
with her young sisters.
Suddenly, she saw a wonderful deer
with eyes like stars...

"Catch me
if you can!"
called the deer.

The princess and her sisters followed after it.
They galloped and galloped
as fast as they could go.
But however fast they went,
the deer was always just ahead.

At last, the poor horses
could go no farther.
"Let's turn back!"
cried Gloriana's sisters.
But Gloriana wouldn't stop.

Finally, the little sisters could go no farther.
"*Please* turn back!"
they called to Gloriana.
But even then,
she would not stop.

On and on she went
until at last
she couldn't even
hear their cries.

At that moment,
the deer stood still
and waited.
She ran toward it.
"I am a magician,"
said the deer.
"Do you have
any wishes?"

"Oh yes!" cried Gloriana.
"I want to be rich
and live in a splendid castle
with fine, new clothes
and jewels."
"What about your sisters?"
asked the deer.
"I heard them calling you."
"Never mind my sisters,"
said Gloriana,
"they're always calling me
and running after me.
This time, let them find
their own way home."

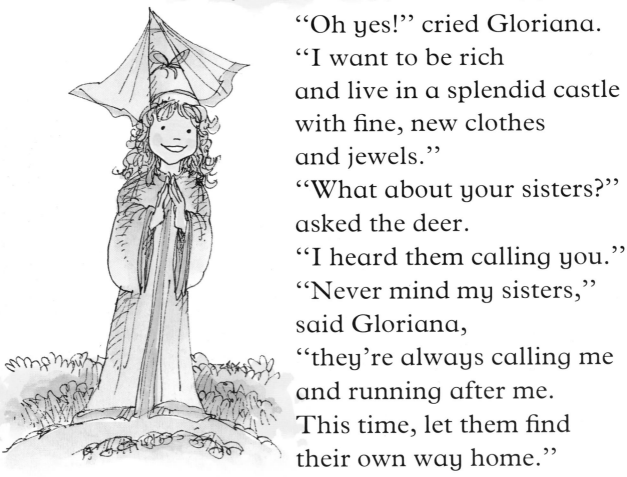

"Very well then,"
said the deer.
"You have your wish.
But someday, *you* will call,
and they won't hear.
Oh, my dear,
you will
cry and cry,
until you are as kind
as you are beautiful."

Suddenly, the deer was gone,
and Gloriana stood on the steps
of a shining castle.

That night,
Gloriana ate from a golden plate
and drank from a golden cup.
She went to sleep
in a golden bed
as big as a boat.

When she woke up,
she found rooms full of jewels
and rich new clothes.
Now she had everything
she wanted –
but there was no one
to see it,
and no one
to share it with.

Time went by.
Soon the splendid castle
seemed very lonely.
One day, Gloriana said,
"I'll ask my sisters
to come and stay with me.
They always do what I want."
Away she went
along the mountain road.

At last, she saw her sisters
in a meadow.
"Sisters, sisters, come with me!"
she cried.
She jumped off her horse
to run to them.

But as soon as her foot
touched the ground,
she turned into
a small, gray rabbit.

"Look! What a dear little rabbit!"
cried her sisters.
As they played with her,
she tried to talk to them,
but they couldn't hear
a single word.

Just **before** sunset,
they **waved** goodbye
and **went** away.

As **soon as** they had gone,
Gloriana became a princess
once **again**.
But **it was** too late.
She **had** to go back alone
to **her grand** castle.
"**That** mountain must be
bewitched!"
said Gloriana.
The next day,
away she went,
by the river road.

This time, she saw her sisters
by the river bank.
"Sisters, sisters, come with me!"
she cried.
Again, she jumped off her horse
to run to them.
But as soon as her foot
touched the river bank,
she turned into
a little golden fish.
"Look! What a pretty fish!"
cried her sisters.
They leaned out over the river
to try to see her.
She leaped high
to try to speak to them.
But of course,
they couldn't hear
a single word.

This time,
Gloriana cried
and cried,
but her tears
ran into the river,
and no one saw them.

At sunset,
her sisters went away.
Once again,
Gloriana went back alone
to her grand castle.
"Perhaps the river
is bewitched,"
said Gloriana.
So the next day
she rode
into the forest.

The forest was dark
and gloomy.
Gloriana
was frightened.
But
she
went
on.

Suddenly, the wonderful deer
ran across her path.
Her sisters came chasing after it
with a hunter.

They were galloping, galloping,
straight toward a cliff.

"Stop! Stop!"
called Gloriana.
She jumped
from her horse
to stand in front of them.
But this time
she turned into
a great white bear.
And when she called,
her voice was a great roar.

They stopped –
and the hunter raised his bow
and shot her.

Down fell the bear,
still roaring.
As it fell,
its roar became
the sweet voice
of the princess.

The hunter raised his bow
to shoot again.
But
the little princesses
heard their sister's voice.
"No!" they cried.
"Don't shoot!
It's Gloriana!"
They ran to hug
the wounded bear,
and its eyes filled
with tears.

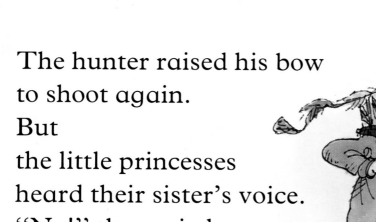

Then a voice said,
"Don't cry, Gloriana."
There stood
the wonderful deer
with eyes like stars.
It said,
"You risked your life
to save your sisters –
you have become as kind
as you are beautiful."

As it spoke,
Gloriana again became
a princess.

Then, suddenly,
the deer was gone
and the sisters stood
on the steps of the shining castle
where they stayed together,
all their long and happy lives.